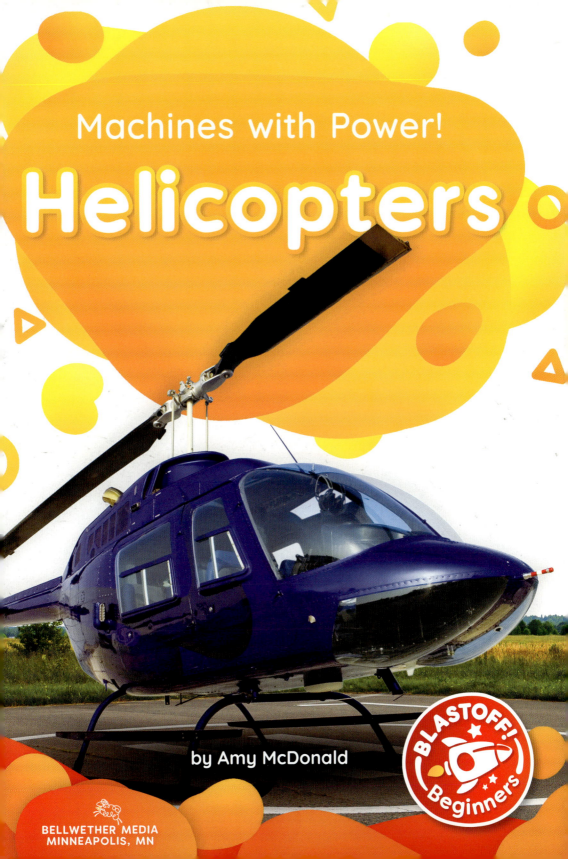

Machines with Power!

Helicopters

by Amy McDonald

BELLWETHER MEDIA • MINNEAPOLIS, MN

Blastoff! Beginners are developed by literacy experts and educators to meet the needs of early readers. These engaging informational texts support young children as they begin reading about their world. Through simple language and high frequency words paired with crisp, colorful photos, Blastoff! Beginners launch young readers into the universe of independent reading.

Sight Words in This Book

a	help	one	these	what
are	here	people	they	you
do	is	see	this	
down	it	sit	to	
for	look	that	up	
has	on	the	water	

This edition first published in 2022 by Bellwether Media, Inc.

No part of this publication may be reproduced in whole or in part without written permission of the publisher. For information regarding permission, write to Bellwether Media, Inc., Attention: Permissions Department, 6012 Blue Circle Drive, Minnetonka, MN 55343.

Library of Congress Cataloging-in-Publication Data

Names: McDonald, Amy, author.
Title: Helicopters / by Amy McDonald.
Description: Minneapolis, MN : Bellwether Media, Inc., 2022. | Series: Machines with power! | Includes bibliographical references and index. | Audience: Ages 4-7 | Audience: Grades K-1
Identifiers: LCCN 2021003768 (print) | LCCN 2021003769 (ebook) | ISBN 9781644874769 (library binding) | ISBN 9781648343841 (ebook)
Subjects: LCSH: Helicopters--Juvenile literature.
Classification: LCC TL716.2 .M33 2022 (print) | LCC TL716.2 (ebook) | DDC 629.133/352--dc23
LC record available at https://lccn.loc.gov/2021003768
LC ebook record available at https://lccn.loc.gov/2021003769

Text copyright © 2022 by Bellwether Media, Inc. BLASTOFF! BEGINNERS and associated logos are trademarks and/or registered trademarks of Bellwether Media, Inc.

Editor: Christina Leaf   Designer: Andrea Schneider

Printed in the United States of America, North Mankato, MN.

Table of Contents

What Are Helicopters?	4
Parts of a Helicopter	8
Helicopters at Work	14
Helicopter Facts	22
Glossary	23
To Learn More	24
Index	24

What Are Helicopters?

Look up!
What do you see?
A helicopter!

Helicopters are machines that fly.

Parts of a Helicopter

This is a **rotor**.
Its **blades** spin.

rotor

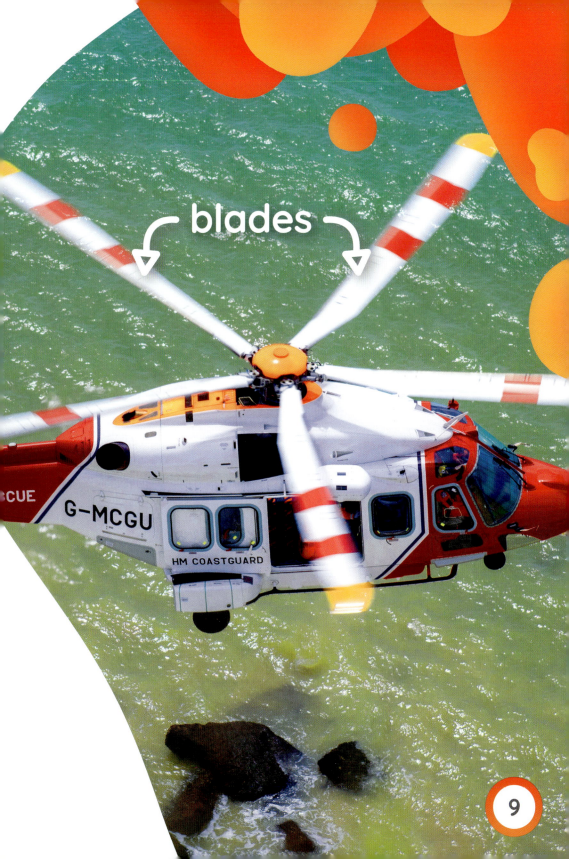

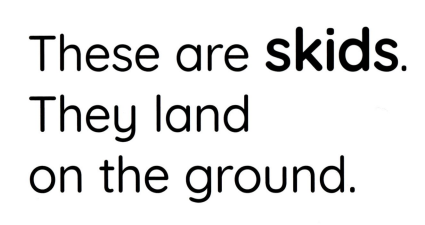

These are **skids**.
They land
on the ground.

This is the **cockpit**. People sit here.

cockpit

Helicopters at Work

This helicopter is for TV.
It has a camera.

This one fights fires.
It drops water.

This one goes to the hospital. It helps people.

This one is just for fun! Look down!

Helicopter Facts

Helicopter Parts

rotor
blades
skids
cockpit

Helicopter Jobs

fight fires

move sick people

take tours

Glossary

blades

parts of a rotor that spin

cockpit

the part of a helicopter where people sit

rotor

the part of a helicopter that helps it fly

skids

the landing feet of a helicopter

To Learn More

ON THE WEB

FACTSURFER

Factsurfer.com gives you a safe, fun way to find more information.

1. Go to www.factsurfer.com.

2. Enter "helicopters" into the search box and click 🔍.

3. Select your book cover to see a list of related content.

Index

blades, 8, 9
camera, 14, 15
cockpit, 12
fires, 16
fly, 6
fun, 20
ground, 10
hospital, 18
land, 10

machines, 6
people, 12, 18
rotor, 8
sit, 12
skids, 10, 11
spin, 8
TV, 14
water, 16

The images in this book are reproduced through the courtesy of: Ponomaryov Vlad, front cover; Photos SS, pp. 3, 22 (helicopter parts); Roman Babakin, pp. 4-5; Irina Montero, pp. 6-7; Iakov Filimonov, p. 8; Duncan Cuthbertson, pp. 8-9; Moshe Einhorn, pp. 10-11; Mauizio Milanesio, p. 12; S-F, pp. 12-13; Brett Barnhill, pp. 14-15; Valeev, p. 16; FCG, pp. 16-17; Robert Convery/ Alamy, pp. 18-19; Image Professionals GmbH/ Alamy, pp. 20-21; smikeymikey1, p. 22 (fight fires); Monkey Business Images, p. 22 (move sick people); lassedesignen, p. 22 (take tours); Aerovista Luchtfotografie, p. 23 (blades); Nattapon B, p. 23 (cockpit); Anupong Nantha, p. 23 (rotor); Makushin Alexey, p. 23 (skids).